Molly McBride and the Party Invitation

A Story About the Virtue of Charity

Text and illustrations by
Jean Schoonover-Egolf

Our Sunday Visitor
Huntington, Indiana
www.osv.com

For my family.
May charity and love prevail.

Molly McBride #3
Molly McBride and the Party Invitation
Copyright © 2019, 2018 by Jean Schoonover-Egolf.

Edited by Jerry Windley-Daoust. Proofreading by Karen Carpenter.

24 23 22 21 20 19   2 3 4 5 6 7 8 9

ISBN: 978-1-68192-507-3 (Inventory No. T2396)
LCCN: 2019939985

Our Sunday Visitor Publishing Division
Our Sunday Visitor, Inc.
200 Noll Plaza
Huntington, IN 46750
1-800-348-2440

**More fun with
Molly McBride!**

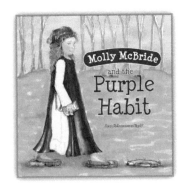

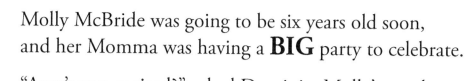

Molly McBride was going to be six years old soon, and her Momma was having a **BIG** party to celebrate.

"Aren't you excited?" asked Dominic, Molly's good friend. "Your party is in **ONE WEEK**!"

"Yes, I am excited," Molly said glumly. "Except for one problem."

"What problem?"

"The name of my problem is **SAM**," Molly sighed. "Momma says I have to invite **EVERYONE** in our class, because we have to 'be kind and show charity.' Except I **DO NOT** want to invite that Sam."

"Oh…Sam!" Dominic said, nodding.

Sam was mean to **EVERYBODY**.

Sam was **NOT** kind.

Sam did **NOT** act like he had charity in his heart!

Sam cut in line at lunch. He wouldn't share the ball with anyone else on the playground. And he made fun of Molly's purple bandana and Dominic's priest collar.

(Molly wore her purple bandana along with her school uniform because she wasn't allowed to wear her purple habit to school. And Dominic wore his priest collar with his school uniform because he had to leave his blacks at home.)

Molly thumbed through the stack of invitations in her lap. She just couldn't let that mean guy ruin her party!

She pulled out one envelope.

"Maybe I could lose this one," she whispered to Dominic. She felt a funny feeling in her stomach.

Dominic got a funny feeling in his stomach, too. But he heard himself say, "Give me mine. . . and Sam's."

"Did you pass out your invitations today, Molly?" Momma asked after school.

Molly's heart went **flippity-flop**.

She fidgeted and then answered, "Um, not yet."

Francis gave out a little yelp because Molly accidentally squeezed him.

"Why not?" Daddy asked. "Was there a problem?"

"I'll do it Monday, Daddy,"
Molly promised.

Molly McBride had a hard time sleeping that night.

Thoughts kept bothering her. And a very icky feeling.

It made Francis have a hard time sleeping, too.

The next day was Saturday, but Molly didn't hop out of bed quite as happily as usual. "We have a special day planned with the Children of Mary sisters," Momma reminded her.

But even that good news didn't make Molly feel better.

In the car, Momma shared her plans for the birthday party: the chocolate-and-vanilla marble cake, the vanilla ice cream, the colorful streamers, the party games.

But Molly didn't want to talk about the party. Talking about the party reminded her about Sam. She thought that she had solved her "Sam problem." If he didn't get the invitation, he wouldn't be at the party.

But then why did she still feel so icky inside?

"Molly," Momma said, "how are things going with that tall boy in your class, the one who was giving some of the kids a hard time?"

"Oh, Momma!" Molly burst out. "Sam's just awful!
Yesterday he bumped into Elizabeth on purpose to
make her drop her cookie! And he grabbed David's
scarf and threw it over the fence! He's so **mean**!"

"Hmm. Well, I will talk with his parents when they come over to our house for the birthday party."

The icky feeling in Molly's stomach suddenly got much ickier.

At last they arrived at the convent where the Children of Mary sisters lived. The McBrides, along with some other families, came here once a month to volunteer for *Ora et Labora* ("Pray and Work.")

"It's a chance to practice **charity**," Daddy said cheerfully.

Well, this was one act of charity Molly really liked doing. She loved helping her friends, the Children of Mary sisters.

Mother Margaret Mary spoke to the families already gathered in the sisters' little chapel to begin their day of *Ora et Labora.*

When they walked into the chapel, Molly was glad to see that Dominic was already there with his family, the Romanos. (His family made him do charity, too.)

As they prayed the Rosary together, Molly prayed a little prayer of her own: *Help me be happy again!*

After the Rosary, Molly and Dominic were assigned to help sweep the walkways outside.

They were hard at work when they heard a familiar voice.

"Well, if it isn't my good friends Miss Molly and Mr. Dominic!" exclaimed Father Matt.

Father explained that he often came to the convent to pray about what he would say during his homily at Mass.

"I had an easy time this week," he said. "The Gospel story is about Jesus going to a party with some not-so-nice guests."

"Well," Father Matt said, "Jesus picked Matthew to be one of his apostles, even though everyone hated him."

"Why did they hate him?" Molly asked.

"Because he was a tax collector. He took the people's money, kept some of it for himself, and gave some of it to their enemies, the Romans."

"That's not very nice," Dominic said.

"Well, then Matthew invited Jesus to a party at his house," Father Matt explained. "And there were even more not-so-nice people at the party."

"The Pharisees and the high priests didn't understand why Jesus would want to be at a party with such unlikeable folks. They thought he should only hang out with nice people like them— people who prayed a lot and were always good."

"But why would Jesus go to a party with people nobody likes?" Dominic asked.

"There are many stories in the Gospel about Jesus being kind to people no one else liked," Father Matt said. "People who were very sick, like lepers, and people who had done bad things."

"Like the woman at the well!"
Molly exclaimed. "Jesus wasn't s'pose to talk
to her because…um, I forget why."

"That's right," laughed Father Matt. "She was a Samaritan woman,
and Jews weren't even allowed to use a cup or a plate if a Samaritan
had touched it. And there was Our Lord, asking that woman for a
drink as she drew up water from the well."

Dominic nodded. "That's because Jesus said we're supposed to even love our enemies, an' he did that—he forgave those guys who put him on the cross!"

"That's right," Father Matt said. "Ever wonder why it is much easier to be charitable to our friends than our enemies? But with Jesus' help, we can love even our enemies!"

Then Molly's eyes brightened.

"Father Matt," Molly said, "I need to go talk to my mom. Can you help Dominic finish sweeping?"

Molly told Momma the whole truth. And when Momma gave her a big hug, she realized she felt happy again on the inside. *Thank you, Jesus,* she whispered.

On their way home, the McBrides did one more act of charity: they delivered a certain "lost" invitation.

The next Saturday, Molly's house was **HOPPING** with kids. With her heart full of charity, she approached Sam with a big smile. "I'm so glad you could make it, Sam."

Sam smiled back. "Thanks for inviting me, Molly McBride."